THE LAB RATS OF DOCTOR ECLAIR

by

John Bianchi

Welcome to the University of Mont Foozle. I'm Lab Rat 99999, but everyone calls me "Niner." I work with the amazing Doctor Eclair, one of the kindest scientists in the whole world. My friends and I have helped him with his experiments for years, but it took a single lightning bolt to make life in the laboratory *really* interesting.

Mind you, before that storm, things were already pretty good.

Doctor Eclair never put us into a maze without a map and a compass.

His tests were full of easy multiple-choice questions.

And he always gave us plenty of sports drinks whenever we exercised in our wheel.

But then the lightning bolt struck, and it changed our lab-rat lives forever.

It must have rearranged our molecules, because three of us developed strange new powers.

Ramelda's eyes could shine like lasers.

Blobber's body became incredibly elastic.

And I turned into the biggest, strongest lab rat on Earth.

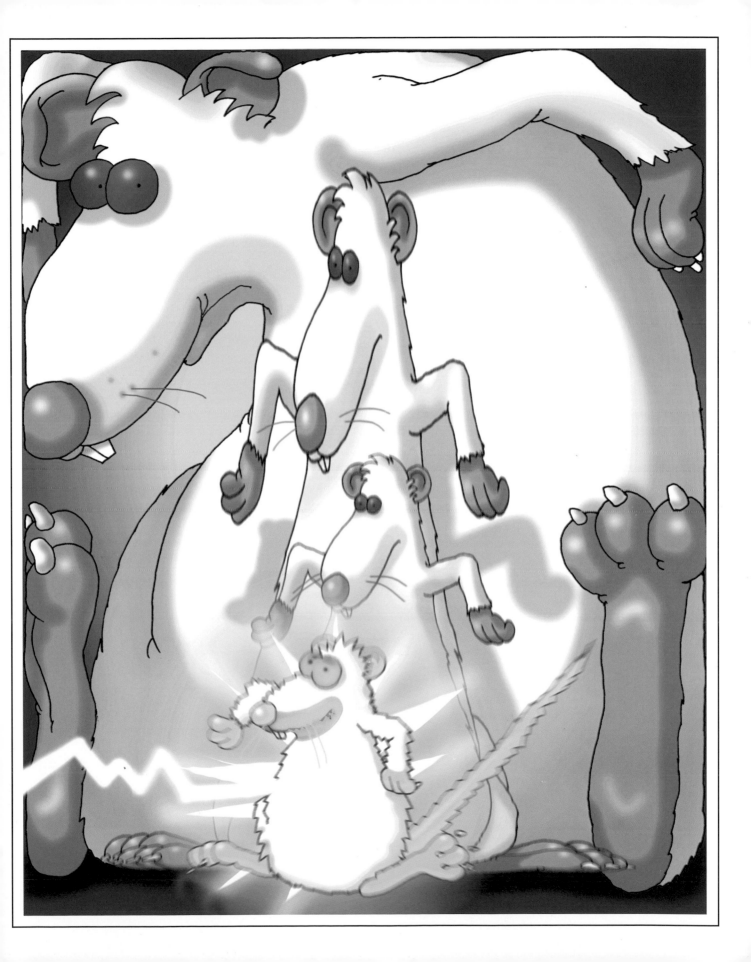

We had to use our new powers immediately. The lightning had started a fire in Doctor Eclair's office, and we rushed to save him!

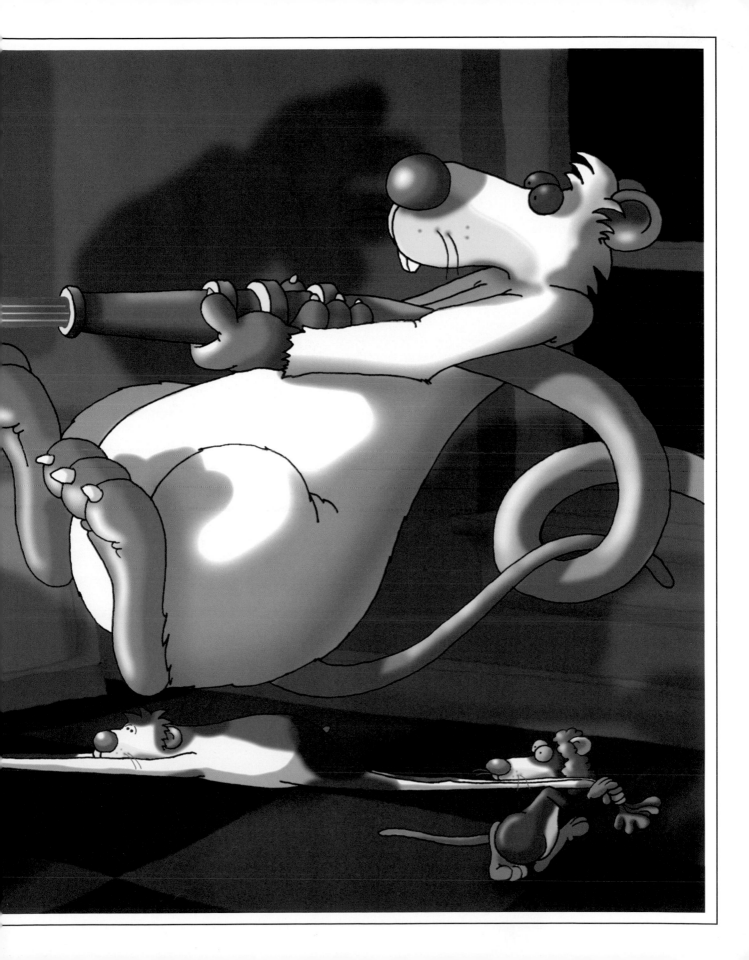

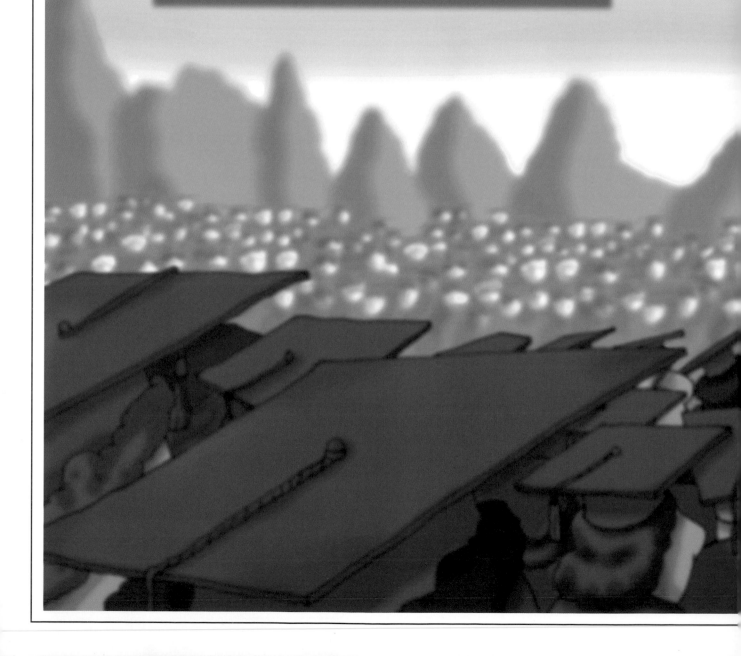

Doctor Eclair was so grateful that he gave us each a medal for our bravery and a diploma for our quick thinking. We were also named Rodents of the Order of Science. During the ceremony, Doctor Eclair announced that he would devote the rest of his life to helping research animals the world over. Together, we would build the first artificial lab rat.

Our early work did not meet with much success. Code-named "WingNut," the prototype was far too big and, unlike real lab rats, not very smart.

To gain a better understanding of rat-brain development, Ramelda offered Doctor Eclair the help of her three ratlings: Zooster, Beamer and Blur.

It was a good theory, but a bad idea. Most days, the ratlings were not very helpful. Some days, we almost wished they would go away. Then one day, they did! Ramelda couldn't find them anywhere.

Doctor Eclair automatically launched a RatScape search, but the computer suggested thousands of possible sites. There was no more time to waste! Ramelda, Blobber and I knew that technology could not replace good old-fashioned legwork. All that maze running and wheel jogging was finally going to pay off!

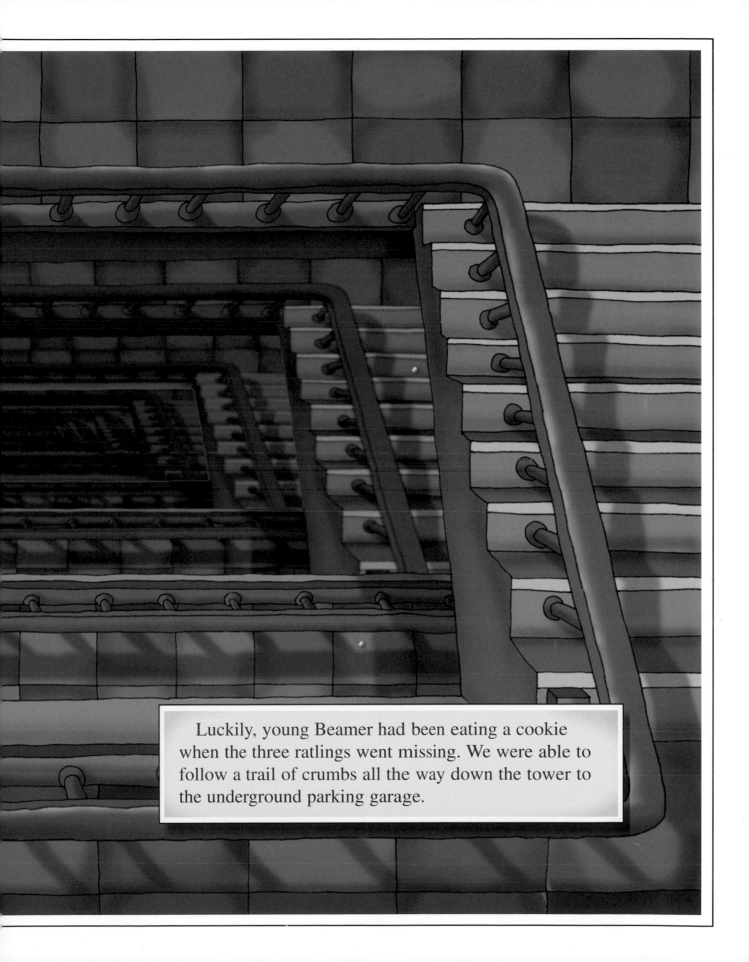

Luckily, young Beamer had been eating a cookie when the three ratlings went missing. We were able to follow a trail of crumbs all the way down the tower to the underground parking garage.

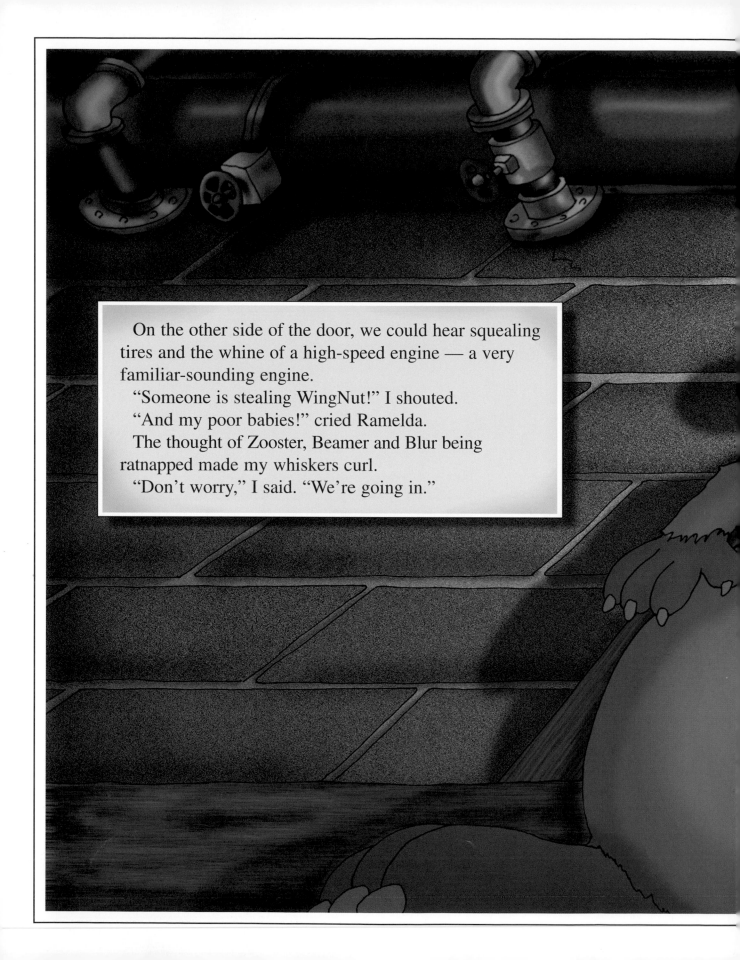

On the other side of the door, we could hear squealing tires and the whine of a high-speed engine — a very familiar-sounding engine.

"Someone is stealing WingNut!" I shouted.

"And my poor babies!" cried Ramelda.

The thought of Zooster, Beamer and Blur being ratnapped made my whiskers curl.

"Don't worry," I said. "We're going in."

Inside, the garage floor trembled under our feet as we struggled through a dense cloud of high-octane exhaust.

Ramelda scanned ahead while we felt our way through the smog. As we advanced closer to the source of the racket, we suddenly stopped and gasped.

We could hardly believe our eyes.

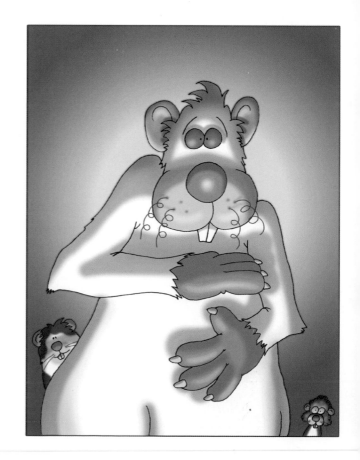

The rat brats had taught WingNut how to play tail-tag, and now the troublesome tin rat was racing out of control, screeching around the parking garage, going faster and faster with each turn. We had to act quickly.

There is only one way to catch a giant tin rat.

I grabbed some metal pipes, and using all our powers — and some of Blobber's cheese for bait — we set to work.

When we were finished, we shoved our giant-tin-rat trap into the path of Doctor Eclair's unruly rodent.

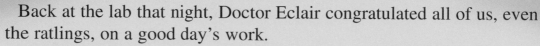

Back at the lab that night, Doctor Eclair congratulated all of us, even the ratlings, on a good day's work.

"By joining the ratlings at play," he explained, "WingNut has shown the first true signs of rat-brain development. He may now be ready for a real scientific test." Doctor Eclair then gave us something to dream about — a daring plan to land WingNut on Jupiter's frozen moon Europa.

"Cool," I thought. "Very cool."

The way WingNut's small brain was
working, I knew Ramelda, Blobber and
I would be going along for the ride.